....

Princess
Posy

Contents

igloobooks

Published in 2015
by Igloo Books Ltd
Cottage Farm
Sywell
NN6 0BJ
www.igloobooks.com

LEO002 1214
2 4 6 8 10 9 7 5 3 1
ISBN: 978-1-78440-177-1

Illustrated by Amanda Enright

Printed and manufactured in China

Princess Stories

igloobooks

Princess Crystal's Cleaner-Upper

Princess Crystal loved to invent things. "I wish I could invent something to stop my family being so very untidy," she thought, one day. "It's the Royal Ball tonight and I'm worried the guests will think the palace is a mess."

There were muddy footprints on the carpet, towels on the banister and cobwebs everywhere. "No one will help me clean this up," Crystal whispered. "They're too lazy. I need to invent something to clean this mess faster than I could."

5

Crystal decided to invent a Cleaner-Upper. The problem was, her strange inventions didn't always work as they were meant to. The Sunshine Maker had made it rain for three weeks and The Automatic Weeder had ripped out the queen's roses and she wasn't happy about it.

Princess Crystal took the Cleaner-Upper to the kitchen and turned it on. It roared into action, wiping up crumbs, washing dishes and sweeping up cobwebs. Crystal was delighted with it. "The Cleaner-Upper will make everything neat and tidy before the guests arrive tonight," she said.

In the ballroom, The Cleaner-Upper cleaned the floor and
the chandeliers at the same time. Crystal watched happily until
suddenly, it started to shudder and rumble. Then, there was a
loud bang. Clouds of smoke filled the ballroom.

"Oh, no," said Crystal, feeling very unhappy. "Now I'll never get the ballroom cleaned up in time," and she began to cry.

Just then, the rest of the royal family came running in. "Sorry we've all been so lazy," they said. "We'll help to clean up." Immediately, the queen started sweeping and the king began polishing. Even Crystal's little brother and sister joined in.

Everyone cleaned and tidied the ballroom. Just as they were
putting their brooms and dusters away, the first guests arrived.
The queen straightened her crown and brushed crumbs off the
king's robe. The prince shook a cobweb out of his hair and the
princesses dusted down their dresses.

The band played and everyone danced and chatted.
Crystal admired the sparkling ballroom. "The Cleaner-Upper
was a bit of a disaster, but I learned something important,"
she said. "To get things done you don't need inventions,
you just need teamwork."

Princess Tiffany's Trumpet

There was a terrible noise coming from the pink palace. The royal unicorns galloped away in fright, the royal pigeons flew off and even the dragon that lived nearby put his paws over his ears. The reason for the noise was Princess Tiffany. She was playing her trumpet.

Tiffany played the piano, the harp and the electric guitar too, but she loved playing her trumpet most of all. The only problem was that she wasn't very good at it. "The more I play, the better I'll get," said Tiffany. "I bet Mum would love to hear me play." Tiffany set off to search for the queen.

The queen was having a nap on her throne when Princess
Tiffany burst in and blew on her trumpet. "Oh, my!" cried the
queen, almost falling off the throne. "That trumpet is too noisy,
Tiffany, please go and play in the tower so I can have my nap
in peace and quiet."
"Sorry, Mum," said Princess Tiffany, as she trudged away.

In the tower, Tiffany heard a tooting noise. "Dad's playing with his train set again," she said. "I can make a better sound than that." She pushed open the door and blasted a note on her trumpet. The king was so surprised that he crashed his model train. "No trumpets in here, Tiffany," he said. "Please play outside instead."

Outside, Princess Tiffany's brother, Prince Henry, was painting a picture of the royal fountain. Tiffany blew a note on her trumpet so loudly, it frightened the prince. "You made me jump with that racket," he shouted, accidentally swishing paint across his picture. "Go away, Tiffany."

Just then, the royal gardener arrived with some beautiful flowers for planting. "I'll paint those instead," said the prince, glaring at Tiffany. "As my other picture was ruined."

"Don't worry, Princess," said the gardener, kindly. "I know where you can play." Tiffany followed him to the kitchen garden where the vegetables grew.

"You won't disturb anyone here," the gardener told her. "There are just those cheeky birds pecking at my plants and seeds. They're not even frightened by my scarecrow."

Tiffany smiled. "I think I can help you with that," she said and blew a thunderous blast on her trumpet, causing the birds to fly away in fright.

When all the birds had gone, Tiffany sat down on a bench with the gardener who produced a box of juicy strawberries.

"If not for you, the birds would have got these," he said.

"You can play here whenever you like."

Tiffany was very happy. Now she could make as much noise as she wanted and no one would ever complain again!

A Princess Surprise

It was Princess Posy's birthday and she was very excited. She jumped out of bed and ran quickly downstairs to the breakfast room, but no one was around. "Maybe they've forgotten my birthday," thought Posy. She poured herself some cereal and saw a golden envelope with her name on it. Excitedly, Posy opened the envelope and read the note inside.

'Eat your breakfast, then head for the place where you clean your teeth and wash your face.'

"It's a treasure hunt," cried Posy and she rushed off to the palace bathroom to find the next clue

Princess Posy

Posy searched the bathroom and found the clue hidden behind her toothpaste pot, by the window.

*'When your teeth are clean, don't stop to rest.
Skip to the place where you get dressed.'*

So, Posy brushed her teeth so they were nice and clean, then rushed off to the dressing room.

In the royal dressing room, Posy found the most beautiful
dress ever. She put it on and twirled around. As she did, another
clue fell from the pocket.

'Climb to the top of the treasury tower.
There you'll find a special flower.'

Posy ran to the top room of the tower, where the royal
jewels were kept and looked around. On a velvet cushion
was a flower hairclip. Posy smiled and put it in her hair.

Just then, she spotted something under the cushion.
"I bet I can guess what's in this envelope," she said.

Posy opened it and read the clue, but it was a bit confusing.

'Now climb on board and close your eyes.
Eight legs will take you to a surprise.'

Suddenly, Posy heard a neighing sound and a clip-clop of hooves coming from outside.

A royal carriage pulled by two horses took Posy to the
royal gardens, where the king and queen were waiting.
Her best friend, Princess Polly was there, too. "Surprise!"
they cried. "Happy Birthday, Posy."

There was a chest full of wonderful presents and the royal cook had made a delicious birthday cake with stripey candles on top. "Thank you so much," said Posy. "I'm so lucky to have such a kind family and a brilliant birthday surprise."

Princess Bella's First Day

It was Princess Bella's first day at Royal School and she was feeling nervous. "I wish I had some friends," thought Bella, sadly. "What if no one talks to me all day?" She didn't know anyone and she felt too shy to ask anyone to play.

Bella walked towards the entrance of the school. Her tummy felt like it had butterflies in it. She could see other children talking and laughing, but they didn't seem to notice her. She began to feel like crying. "I don't think I like school," she thought. Just then, the bell rang. It was time to line up and go inside.

Lessons were fun and the morning passed quickly, but Bella wasn't looking forward to play time. "I don't want to be alone," she thought. She was watching the other children playing when she heard a friendly voice. "Hello, I'm princess Wendy, would you like to play with me?" said a kind-looking girl.

The two new friends giggled as they played on the climbing frame. They skipped and played together. "Let's ask some more girls to join in," said Wendy. "It'll be fun." Bella wasn't sure, but Wendy soon introduced her to more of her friends and Bella loved it. "I think I do like school after all," she said, happily.

While Bella was playing with her new friends, she noticed a little girl sitting alone. "She looks sad," Bella thought, skipping over to join her. "Come and play with us," said Bella and the girl smiled happily.

"I'd love to," the girl said. "My name's Paige."

"You'll soon have lots of friends to play with," Bella said.

Bella introduced Paige to Wendy and the other girls and
before long they were all having a great time singing and skipping
together. They quickly became the best of friends.
"It's good to be friendly when you meet someone new,"
said Bella. "Now I can say I enjoyed my first day at school."

33

Princess Arabella's New Kite

Princess Arabella was very excited. She'd been waiting for a windy day for ages, so she could fly her new kite. "My kite will fly higher than the palace tower," she said. Her little sister, Jennifer, asked if she could play too, but Arabella was too excited to listen and ran off.

After several tries, Arabella finally got the kite to fly. It swooped and soared in the wind, with its tail swirling along behind. She tugged on the kite's string, making it dip and dance, but the kite flew higher until she could hardly hold on to it.

A strong gust of wind suddenly caught the kite and blew it into an apple tree. Arabella tried to pull it free, but it was well and truly stuck.. "Shall I help?" Princess Jennifer asked. "No thanks, I can do it on my own," said Arabella and she managed to pull the kite free at last.

Princess Arabella started to fly her kite again. It looped and flashed through the air as the wind blew it and again Arabella had trouble holding onto the string. "Do you need some help?" Princess Jennifer asked.

"No thanks," Arabella muttered. "I can manage." However, as she spoke the string broke and the kite soared up into the sky.

Watching her kite disappear into the distance, Arabella wiped a tear from her cheek. Seeing how upset her sister was, Princess Jennifer went over and put an arm around her.

"We can make a better kite together," Jennifer said. So, the two sisters collected everything they needed to make a new kite and when they'd finished it looked amazing.

That afternoon, the two princesses flew their brilliant new
kite together. It soared high and floated on the breeze,
long streamers waving and sequins sparkling in the sunlight.
"It's much more fun playing together," Arabella said.
"Now we have an amazing kite to share with each other,"
Jennifer said, smiling.

The Spoilt Princess

Once, there was a princess who had a fairy godmother.
Whatever the princess wanted her fairy godmother gave to her.
However, the spoilt princess never said please or thank you.
"I want a thousand cupcakes," demanded the princess.
So, her fairy godmother made them appear, but the princess
took a bite of one and tossed it away.

Next, the princess asked for a purple dragon. The fairy
godmother made it appear, but when flames shot from its nose,
the princess screamed in fright. "Make it go away," she wailed.

When the spoilt princess asked for a new dress, the fairy godmother conjured up a beautiful, sequined yellow gown. "I wanted a pink dress, not a yellow one," the princess said.

The fairy godmother was beginning to feel tired, but she waved her wand and the dress turned pink.

The pink dress was beautiful, but suddenly the princess spotted a blue bird on the lawn. "Change the dress to blue," she said. "I mean red. No, I mean stripes."

The princess kept changing her mind over and over. "I want a dress like a rainbow, with every colour in it," she demanded.

The dress changed colour at incredible speed. First one then another and another. Finally, there was a loud pop and the dress began to fall to pieces. "What's happening?" the princess demanded.

The fairy godmother flopped down. Her cloak was ripped, her broken wand dangling uselessly. "Too much magic," she sighed and fell into a deep sleep.

Looking at her sleeping fairy godmother's face and frazzled hair, the princess felt guilty. "She's always been kind to me and I've been so selfish," she said. "I don't know how to mend a broken wand, but I will show her how sorry I am."

The princess picked up the pieces of her dress and ran into the palace.

Working as fast as she could, the princess stitched the scraps of material together to make a beautiful new cloak. When the fairy godmother woke up she was so happy. "It's beautiful," she sighed, putting on the patchwork cloak and twirling around.

"It's so much prettier than my old cloak. You are very clever, Princess."

"I'm sorry for being so selfish and spoilt," said the princess smiling. The fairy godmother was so pleased with the princess, she quickly repaired her new wand and waved it. A tiara popped onto the princess's head.
"Now we can both wear something beautiful," the fairy godmother said and for the very first time, the princess actually said thank you!